Zack'S Tales-Travels of A Guide Dog

the real author!

ZACK

To order additional copies, please contact us.
BookSurge, LLC
www.booksurge.com
1-866-308-6235
orders@booksurge.com

Zack'S Tales-Travels of A Guide Dog

Zack's Tales

Audrey M. Gunter

2004

Zack'S Tales-Travels of A Guide Dog

Zack's Tales
Travels of a Guide Dog

Told by **me**, Zack, the very best guide dog in the world, and written by my mom in a language only we can understand

This book, written with love, is dedicated to those very special people mentioned within. Each has made a huge impact on our lives with their support, care and influence, especially the Puppy Raisers.

Your unselfishness and generosity have touched so many lives. Everything constructive that we achieve, is a direct result of your efforts. Please know that through what you do our dignity is restored. You give the blind a chance to once again enjoy a personal independence they'd only dreamed about.

A very special "thank you" is offered to Zack's Puppy Raisers. Cheri and Lew have been, are and will always be a very big part of our lives. Thank you for caring so much.

MY BEGINNING

Hello, everyone!

I've been doing a lot of listening and watching you human folks and you have it all wrong. You guys think you are so smart. Well, you obviously haven't met all my buddies and me.

You see, I'm *special*. I was *specially born* to be special. My *mom and dad* were special and all *my brothers and sisters* are special too. There are millions and millions of you human guys; but only a few thousand of us! You see I'm a specially bred, specially born, specially raised, specially trained service dog called a **GUIDE DOG!**

EARLY DAYS

I was born in Palmetto, Florida, on November 26, 2000, at Southeastern Guide Dog School. All 8 of my brothers and sisters were black, like my mom, Judy. I was the only yellow lab in the litter, like my dad, Walker. When it came time to leave the nursery at Southeastern, my brothers and sisters all went to a prison I.M.P.A.C.T. Program to be raised by the inmates. I went to some special folks- Lew & Cheri, who live in a great big house with lots of toys for me to play with, a great big yard for me to run and jump around in; and even a neat pool where I could swim and chase my kongs. I even had a big brother, Mikey, who liked to run and play with me. My big sister, Brie, just wanted to boss both of us around and make sure we knew she was the top dog in the family. Big deal! I didn't care. I just wanted to run and play and swim and, after a long hard day, curl up beside my new mom and dad.

We spent a lot of time together. Momma Cheri and Daddy Lew took me everywhere they went and taught me to do lots and lots of things. I even went to work with them at the hospital in Sarasota. Each morning, after they put on their clothes, they'd dress me in this cool blue vest and off we'd go. I looked good! Everyone loved me, even way back then.

I *was* good, too. My Momma-Cheri and Daddy-Lew always told me what a good boy I was 'specially when I first learned to go to the bathroom outside. They always said I was a "good boy!" The more they said that, the more I'd sit or lie down or stand or heel for them. I loved to hear their praise and they loved to praise me. It was, indeed, an ideal home for any well trained, handsome future guide dog.

After we'd get back home from a long, hard day at Momma-Cheri's office, she'd take my vest off of me and I would get to run and play with Mikey and Brie. Then, we'd all come in for one of my favorite times of the day-dinner! After we ate, we'd go back outside for a nice long walk. Finally, we'd come back home and I would get to curl up beside Momma-Cheri or Daddy-Lew and doze off to sleep. Oh, I wasn't supposed to get on their bed, so I'd patiently wait until they both fell asleep, and then I would quietly jump up and settle down by their feet. When they woke up the next day, they'd fuss a little at me, but I didn't really care. I'd just look up at them with my handsome big brown eyes, cock my head to one side and try to appear so pitiful, as if to say,

"I'm really sorry."

The next night, I'd sneak right back up there.

I lived with my Momma Cheri and Daddy Lew for about fourteen months. When it came time for me to leave home and go to school we all cried. Momma Cheri loved me so much she even wanted to leave the country with me, but she and Daddy Lew tearfully loaded me up in the car and off we went back to Southeastern.

GUIDE DOG SCHOOL

When I got back to the kennels I found all my old buddies had returned too. We were born around the same time and we used to romp and play together over in the puppy section. They'd gotten so big I could hardly recognize them. Seeing them again was really cool and we must have jumped and chased each other all day. We spent the entire day playing together. When it got dark, though, Momma-Cheri and Daddy Lew were no where to be found. I looked everywhere for them.

Where had they gone? Didn't they know they needed me to keep them busy? Who was going to play with Mikey now? Who was going to aggravate Brie? Who was going to jump up on their bed and keep their feet warm tonight? Who were they going to fuss at tomorrow morning? How were they going to get to work without me?

"Okay, you guys! Enough is enough! It's time to go home now. Come on out and get me. I'm tired and I want our bed."

That first night back at the kennels was probably the longest of my life. The concrete floors were hard and there were no nice soft carpets to curl up on. I didn't have much time to complain, though, because almost immediately I began my guide dog training.

Each morning the trainers would come in and load us all up in their vans. Off we'd go! I learned so much! I learned to stop at all curbs and steps and anywhere else that may cause harm to my handler. I learned to recognize elevators, escalators, planters, benches, chairs, mailboxes, trashcans and doors going in and doors going out. I learned that, when I had on my special harness, I needed to guide my trainer around obstacles, low hanging limbs, across streets, through crowds and away from anyone or anything that could cause us harm. I learned to ignore other people and even other dogs. I was so focused on my job that I didn't have time to sniff or grab food that folks had dropped on the ground. I even learned to go to the bathroom on command. I learned my left from my right and what to do if a car or a bicyclist came towards us. Oh, sure! I made a couple of mistakes at first, but I soon got the hang of everything and folks just kept talking about how smart and laid back I was. I was really catching on to all of this guide dog stuff and it wasn't long before I'd completed my training and was ready to be matched.

MY NEW MOM

I remember that day so well! It was a Tuesday and Striker, Leo, Chance, and I had been out at the kennels watching those new guys with the trainers. We all stood around wondering who our new person would be. Leo and Chance wanted an older person-one that would take their time when they walked. They were both very big boys and could, quite truthfully, stand to lose a couple of pounds. They liked to lo-li-gag around and always walked so slowly. Striker hoped for someone who'd love him and allow him to guide them around. He didn't care how slow or fast his person was-he just wanted love. Geborah, the Visla, was always quite active and bounced all over the place. She wanted a young person who she could go everywhere and do everything with. I hadn't thought much about who I'd get. I wanted someone who could keep up with me-someone who would love and appreciate me and, let me play sometimes.

Soon, the kennel assistants came and got us one at a time and we began getting our baths. After we were all spruced up and loaded on the van, away we went to obedience alley. Aaron and Heidi, the trainers, would come get us one-by-one. I didn't think they'd ever pick me. I was getting so nervous I began to pace back and forth in my crate. First they got Bennie; then Chance; then Leo; then Striker. Next was Maya, Cliff, Sully. I was getting more and more concerned. Were they never going to find the right person for me?

" What's up with this? Surely there has to be someone over there for me."

Finally, Aaron came out and slipped the leash into my correction collar! I tried to behave, but I was so excited! Finally, I was going to get a new home! I couldn't wait to get inside that building to meet my new person.

As Aaron and I walked through the big metal door going into the living room, I heard Jim say, "Audrey, call your dog."

I looked all around to try to see who this "Audrey" person was, but there were so many other people there and so many other newly-matched guide dogs with them, I had no idea which way to look.

All of a sudden I heard this female voice, broken with emotion, cry out, "Zackariah, come here!"

***

"Oh, boy!" I had a person! I went running over to her, jumped up in her arms and we held each other for about 5 minutes. I could feel that she was a little nervous-she'd never had a dog before. I could sense she was a little worried-she'd always depended on a sighted guide or her cane. She wasn't sure whether she could learn to depend on me when she walked

"Throw that old cane away! You have me now. You don't need that old thing."

Most importantly, I could feel her love! I knew from the very first moment-the very first lick, and there were many, from the very first encounter that we were a perfect match. Finally, after all those long hard months of special training-I had my very own person! I was so proud.

My new mom was very big and very strong. She just held me close to her breast, like a little baby. Occasionally, she'd brush away that lock of gray hair that kept falling on her forehead, tears streaming down her plump cheeks and dropping off her chin, all the while squeezing me close to her and telling me she loved me. . Heidi came over to us and told my new mom that she'd have to put me down.

***

"What? Put me down? I-I just got here! Can't I hold my new mom just a little bit longer?"

***

In all the excitement, somehow I'd broken her glasses, knocked out her earring and scratched her cheek. She didn't care, though. She loved me anyway. And I loved her too. Oh, boy, did I love her!

We spent the next couple of days getting adjusted to one another. I had to teach her how to walk all over again. Soon, though, my new mom wanted to walk faster than I'd been used to. Heidi showed her how to get me moving and now we "boogity-boogity" everywhere together. My new mom was a little skeptical at first. She just didn't know what all I could do and how well I could do it. The first day we went to Wal-mart's; I guided her all around that store! We went down every aisle in every department. I took her around the standing crowds, the narrow, congested displays and straight up to the lady at the checkout counter. Mom was buying me a new toy and a shedding blade, but there was no price tag on them. I don't think I'll ever forget when that lady behind the register looked at my mom and asked if she read the price posted on the display.

***

" Wow! Don't you know my mom's eyes are broken? Why do you think I'm here ?"

***

Mom just chuckled, like she usually does when someone's ignorance shines through, and shyly told the lady that she was blind.

"You don't look blind," the lady quipped.

I wanted to shout back, "yeah, well you don't look stupid either, but apparently you are!"

✢✢✢

I just sat there, though; like my mom told me; until someone came up to get the prices for us.

After that day at Wal-Mart's my new mom learned to become more and more confident in me. She learned to trust me and I *always* watched out for her. We went through malls, hotels, crowded streets, across 8- lane intersections, and we even went in busy restaurants, where my mom and the others would eat. Of course, I could smell all those good aromas, but I always laid down by my mom's feet. Never once did I misbehave. Never once did I beg for anything off her plate. I was her "little man." Most of the time she'd call me "sweet potato." I liked that.

For the first week or so we could only walk outside on the school grounds in pairs. Mom really enjoyed being outside and I loved taking her there. I remember one Sunday afternoon when Danielle, a 17 year old, asked Mom if we'd go walk the Freedom Trail with her. Mom wasted no time getting me harnessed up and we were soon following them across the street for our walk. The young girl was totally blind in one eye and only 20/400 acuity in the other. We could tell she was somewhat fearful. Mom's vision was bad, but a lot better than Danielle's and she assured her we'd be right behind them.

"Just follow your dog," Mom said. "You'll be fine."

I've always been very careful guiding my mom. She's really tall, so I had to pay particular attention to those low-hanging limbs. It didn't take me long to learn that her limited visual field would cause her to stumble over uneven sidewalks, tree roots, or anything else below her waist. I had to be very careful, indeed, because the Freedom Trail had all those things!

"Don't worry, Mom, "I won't let you trip on anything."

It didn't take us long to reach the "Ear" tree and the two benches facing each other at the end of the trail. It was a beautiful, warm Florida afternoon and Mom and Danielle were really enjoying being outdoors. Geborah and I were pooped, so we just laid down under the benches as they talked.

Mom soon noticed Danielle's tears and asked why she was crying.

"Miss Audrey," she said, "this is the very first time in my life that I've been able to walk outside without having to hold onto someone's arm. Now, I can go by myself!"

The young blind girl's determination and enthusiasm touched my Mom's heart. As she sat there, thinking of all the things that she'd been able to see in her lifetime, she realized the frail young girl was just beginning hers, but would never be able to enjoy the wondrous beauty of this magnificent world.

"What's that noise?" The young girl nodded her head towards a big irrigation pond.

"There's a high chain link fence about 10 feet over with a pond behind it. There are ducks and Geese swimming over there," Mom answered.

Then Mom decided to describe as much of the surrounding scenery to her as she could. She told her about the fence on the other side, and all the dogs that were playing out in the open field.

"Oh, is Geborah's brother or sister out there?"

"I only see a couple of black labs, "Mom answered.
Wondering whether the young girl had ever really seen her own reflection, mom inquired, "Do you know what you like?"

"No, ma'am," she replied rather sheepishly.

Mom thought for a while, trying to best describe the tiny teenager. "Can you tell anything about how Geborah looks?" Mom asked.

"Yes, ma'am. I hold her really close to me in our room and look at her under the light. She's beautiful."

"Well, your hair is auburn, just like hers and your eyes are brown, like hers. As a matter of fact, you both kind of look alike." Mom was laughing and soon had that courageous young girl laughing too. "You are both beautiful."
Mom reached up and pulled one of those funny looking "ears" off the big tree behind us and let the young girl feel it. Mom brought that "ear" home with us as a constant reminder that there are lots of other folks in worse shape than she is.

It was getting dark when we headed back up to the patio. Geborah safely led her mom up the path and I safely guided my mom just behind them. The trainers said that we feel what they feel and they were right. My mom's pride in this young blind girl traveled down my leash as she realized her very first taste of personal independence in just walking outside.

"Please don't cry, Mom. It hurts my heart when you cry."

A couple of weeks passed and we were really learning a lot of stuff. Well, my mom was learning-I already knew it. Friday came and all of us guides had to get another bath in preparation for "Puppy Raiser Saturday." Heidi showed my mom how to bathe me; how to clean my ears and how to brush my teeth. By the end of that day I was exhausted from all that cleaning. I wasn't exactly sure what "Puppy Raiser Saturday" was, but it had to be very special because I could feel the anxiety from my new mom.

PUPPY RAISER DAY

The next morning, we woke up as usual. After we went to the relief area, Mom got dressed and we went to the dining room for her morning coffee and breakfast. Then we finally went out to the patio for my breakfast. Back outside we went where my mom started brushing me again with my new shedding blade.

"Gosh, Mom, you're gonna brush a hole in me!"

After a little while, my mom slipped my harness on me and we began to line up on the patio. Finally, Aaron and Jim came after all of us and we began our trek down the "Puppy Raiser Walk." I was absolutely perfect! Even when Ms. Helen called my name out, I kept right on walking, my fluffy tail up in the air and strutting, like the "little man" my mom calls me. When we got to the blended curb, some of the other guides just slowed down. Not me! I stopped. I didn't want my mom to trip and get hurt. She was too big and she might just fall on me and hurt me too! Oh, no! I couldn't have that.

"Careful here, Mom. Be careful. Use that foot to feel the slight rise in the pavement."

We walked on to the first planter; then, the next. I stopped at every up curb and down curb, like the professional guide dog I'd become. We crossed the streets and returned to the patio area, where my mom removed my harness. As she was putting it back in my closet, Jan came and got us. It was time to go back in to the living room area of the school.

: Big deal! We've been in there lots and lots of times since that first Tuesday we were matched. What is so special about today that we have to go in one at a time, as called?"

Well, let me tell you what was so special! When my mom and I walked through that big door, there were lots of strange people out there. Most were crying and holding on to these other guys' guides.

"What's up with that?"

Then, I heard a familiar voice. No! It couldn't be!

"Hi, I'm Lew and this is my wife, Cheri."

Wow! Momma Cheri and Daddy Lew had come all that way just to see me graduate. Oh, it was so good to see them again! I just couldn't believe it was really them. I jumped up on Daddy Lew and took his arm in my big mouth. I must have gotten too excited because my tooth made his arm bleed a little. I jumped up and loved on Momma Cheri too. We all stood there, just hugging and loving on each other for about 10 minutes. I don't remember what anyone said at that point. Shoot! I really don't think anyone said anything. They couldn't. They were all crying too hard.

Momma Cheri and Daddy Lew had brought me some of my favorite toys from home. They had my special rope, a nylar bone and very special treat-Frosty Paws. They gave my new mom some photos of me and my brothers and sisters nursing on my real mom, Judy. Since I was the only yellow one in the bunch, it wasn't difficult to spot me.

They must have laughed and talked and cried and laughed and talked and cried for a couple of hours. My tail was exhausted from all that wagging I did. I loved seeing Momma Cheri and Daddy Lew again and I showed them how much I really loved my new mom, too. When we all tearfully said good-bye that day, my new mom and I went back to our room and played with all my toys-the ones she'd brought me and the ones Momma Cheri and Daddy Lew delivered that day. Afterwards, I was so tired that I barely remember my new mom going to bed that night. It had, indeed, been a very, very busy day.

My new mom and I completed the next couple of weeks of training with no problems at all. Well, there was that time in Tampa when I saved her life, but that's all.

You see, Uncle Aaron was teaching Mom and Uncle John how to cross over a busy intersection. Uncle Aaron would take one team at a time across the 8-lane street until they were safely on the other side. Mom and I were first. We stood there, waiting for the sound of the traffic parallel to increase and the perpendicular to quiet down. She asked Uncle Aaron if it were safe and he gave her the approval to cross. There were several light and utility poles blocking his vision so he couldn't see that truck turning, but *I did!* Mom gave me the "forward" command but instead, I pushed her and Uncle Aaron back on the sidewalk and firmly positioned my entire body to block my mom from that reckless truck as it turned too sharply and rolled up on the sidewalk at the very spot we'd been standing.

"Praise that dog!" Uncle Aaron shouted, a big grin on his face.

He didn't have to tell Mom, though, because she was already on her knees, my head in her hands as she kept kissing me and repeating,

"Good boy! Very good boy!"

"Whew, that was a close one, Mom! Please be more careful next time."

Mom got sick that last week, but I took very good care of her. She was really nervous just before our final night walk, though. Although my new mom has a little usable vision in the daytime, at night, she is totally blind. She didn't like going out at night and rarely did, until she got me.

Uncle Jim and Aunt Heidi told us to walk with Aunt Hope and her guide Sully, and Aunt Kathleen and Maya.

"Don't worry, Mom. Just follow me! When I stop, use your search foot to see why I stopped. We'll be fine. I'll take good care of you."

And I did, too. In no time we had returned from that dreaded night walk and Mom was packing our things for our trip home. I was really getting excited. She'd told me so much about Aunt Dorace and Aunt Carolyn, Patches, Sallie and Uuggllee. I could hardly wait to meet them. Neither Mom nor I got much sleep that night.

There was something very special about to happen. I could feel my mom's anxiety as it traveled down my leash and through my correction collar. We'd stayed up almost all night packing. My new mom had my very own special suitcase for all my things. Aunt Sheryl had given it to her as a gift and she saved it for me. Mom showed it to me that first Tuesday and called it "Zack's Bag." Only one problem, though. "Zack's Bag" has pictures of cats all over it. Oh, well! I guess I just have to remember that my new mom can't see too well. She probably thought they were guide dogs, like me.

"That's okay, Mom. I like Zack's Bag. It's perfect."

After she got all her old stuff and my valuable toys and bones packed, we finally settled down for the night.

GOING HOME

The next morning my new mom woke me up really early. She had me out in the relief area before 5am.

" Geez, mom! We just went to bed! I'm barely awake. Surely, you can't expect my kidneys to function this early, can you?"

Soon the others were up and suddenly there was a lot of activity going on in that school. James and Maggie and John and Bennie came up and hugged my mom before saying their good-byes. At least, that's what I think they were saying. There was so much crying going on I really don't know what they said. My mom and I kept walking that morning-from the living room to the dining room to the patio to our room and back to the living room! We went into the dining room for mom's breakfast, but she said since I couldn't eat, she couldn't either. She just drank some coffee and I caught a few much-needed winks down and under her chair. We didn't go to the patio this time, though. Jim told my mom it would be better for me if I didn't eat anything until we got home that night.

"What's up with him? I just wonder how he'd like going a day and a half with no dinner? Gosh, that's like 3 weeks in doggie years, isn't it?"

Finally, we went back to our room when Jan came in and said our family was waiting on us.

" Oh boy! I have a *family* and they are waiting to see *me!*" Uh, oh! Here come that darn shedding blade and grooming comb again."

Mom cleaned the "sleepboogers" out of my eyes and away we went to the living room again.

Mom had me sit, then put me down and under her chair when this nice, but very bossy, lady came running up and hugged my mom. She was crying so hard she couldn't even hear my mom tell her not to pet me. At that point I'm not so sure she even cared what my mom said. She was more interested in *me*.

"He's beautiful! Oh, my God, he's absolutely gorgeous!"

She kept shouting that out to everyone and anyone who would listen. She obviously had great taste, but was just as obvious, quite excited. She finally settled down in the chair next to my mom, stroking and feeling on me constantly.

Mom looked at me and said, "Zack, this is your Aunt Dorace."

I kept putting my head in her lap and petting her while she stroked my ears and back. She reached down to kiss my nose and I gave her a very sloppy lick. I would move her hand with my head so I could keep watch on my mom. I loved Aunt Dorace, but I didn't want anything to happen to my mom, you know.

"Hey, Mom, I like Aunt Dorace. She's cool!"

As soon as things quieted down a little, here came another

sobbing lady! This one couldn't talk at all. She just kept on crying.

Mom just laughed and said, "Zack, meet Aunt Carolyn."

I could sense Aunt Carolyn was a very special lady, indeed. I later learned that it was Aunt Carolyn who talked my mom into getting a guide dog in the first place. I knew I liked her immediately.

"Hi, Aunt Carolyn. Thanks for sending me my new mom. Don't you worry one bit, either. She's in good paws now. I'm gonna take very good care of her."

We hung around the school just long enough to say good-bye to everyone. They all cried and promised to telephone each other and keep in touch. Mom was really sad when she had to leave Uncle Paul and Leo. They had become extraordinarily good friends and were always cutting up with the instructors, especially Uncle Chuck. Uncle Paul promised he'd get his wife to drive him and Leo down to Charleston for a visit in the spring. He wanted to see the gardens in bloom and mom promised to take him fishing. With tears streaming down her face and lots of love in her voice, she told everyone good-bye and we were off to my new home.

"So long, everybody! Don't worry! I really love my new mom and she loves me. We'll take very good care of each other. Who knows? Maybe we'll come back someday for a visit."

The trip to Charleston was a long one. Aunt Dorace and Aunt Carolyn rode in the front, while mom and I sat in the back. I laid across the seat with my head in her lap so she wouldn't be scared.

We stopped a few times for them to eat and for me to busy-busy. It began to get dark and I snuggled even closer to my mom because I know she doesn't like the dark.

"Don't worry, Mom. I'm right here."

We stopped at the Cracker Barrel in Georgia about 7pm and it was pitch black outside. Aunt Dorace and Aunt Carolyn came up to help my mom but stopped when they remembered that was *my* job now. My mom put my harness on me and commanded me to "follow" Aunt Dorace. When we walked in that restaurant people gasped and jaws dropped. Those folks had never seen a working man like me before and they couldn't believe how handsome and well behaved I was! Right through that store we went, around displays and groping kids. I was flawless. When the lady led us to the table, I never one time stopped to sniff or grab something off someone's plate. I just stayed right on Aunt Dorace's heels. Even though the restaurant was dark and crowded, my mom walked right next to me, without tripping, stopping or bumping into anyone or thing. Aunt Dorace and Aunt Carolyn started crying again.

" Oh boy! Just what a guy needs! A bunch of blubbering old ladies! Oh, well! At least they are nice blubbering old ladies."

My chest was about to burst with pride as I felt my Mom's courage build. Oh, she was a little hesitant at first, but gradually she began to relax and let me do my job. Boy! What a great job I did, too.

"Good boy, Zack! Very good boy!"

Folks could hear my mom praising me all over that restaurant that night. She didn't care and neither did I. When we're working together neither of us is aware of anyone else around us. It's as though we are part of each other. She's my Mom and I'm her eyes. It's my job to keep her safe.

PATCHES

Finally, after what seemed to be days of riding, but was actually only about 9 hours, we drove up into ZACK'S Yard. That's right! Zack's Yard. We had lots of grass and bushes and trees in Zack's Yard. I tried my best to water each one of them too. My mom walked me around and finally we went inside where I met her-Patches!

Now, don't get me wrong. I've been around cats before. We even had one or two that lived in the kennels there at Southeastern. But I'd never, ever met a cat just like Patches before. She looked okay, as far as cats go. She was a big calico that had obviously been given her way much too often. As soon as we walked in the door, Patches began hissing. I'd never seen anyone do that, so I ventured up closer to get a better look at her. The closer I got, though, the louder she hissed.

"What's wrong with her? Is she nuts or something?"

Mom called Patches her "little girl" and picked her up off the sofa and began kissing on her

"Ugh! Watch out, Mom. She-she must be a wild cat!"

Patches growled at Mom, but Mom didn't care. She kept right on hugging and kissing on her. Each time I'd stick my nose over there to check on Mom, Patches would growl and hiss again.

"Wow! She growls louder than me."

Patches told me that night, in no uncertain terms, that while she might have to share my mom and our house with me, *she* was the boss and I'd better never forget it. I never did. From that point on, we had a mutual agreement. She would never sit in Mom's lap when we went outside the house and I could never sit in her lap when we were inside. Mom loved us both and we both knew it.

TEACHING OTHERS

For the first couple of weeks after we got home I had to be tied down whenever we were inside, as per the trainers' instructions. I didn't like that much, but Mom wanted to continue doing exactly as she'd been taught. Every morning we'd get up, Mom would feed me and take me outside to busy. Then we'd start walking. We must have walked a gazillion miles. Each time, I'd always remember how to guide my mom back home safely. Aunt Dorace would sometimes take us to the mall and to Wal-Mart's in the car. They both depended on me to remember where she parked the car because Aunt Dorace would forget sometimes.

Before long, folks knew me everywhere. Most had never seen a professional guide dog before and they'd want to pet me. Some would even ask. Mom would always tell them very nicely, "please don't pet him. He's working." She'd even explain to them how petting me could create a distraction and result in our getting hurt. Some would listen and comply. Others would just continue to reach for me. Some would even get insulted and stomp off. I couldn't help but wonder if those same folks were so drawn to my mom's white cane when she had to use it.

Once, while walking around in the mall, some men came up and asked,

"Hey, lady. Is that one of them blind dogs?"

Mom just chuckled as she softly replied,

"He's not blind; I am."

"They don't know, " she'd say, "and they don't know that they don't know.' "We just have to educate them. That's all!"

A couple of weeks later a very nice newspaper reporter lady came to our house and wrote an article about us. She took lots of pictures of me and Mom at home and at the mall. She had to run to keep up with us there.

The very next day as Aunt Dorace was reading the paper, she began to laugh and shout.

"Look whose picture is on the front page!"

Mom got tickled as she realized it was us. Yep, right there on the front page was a huge photo of me letting Mom kiss my nose. Aunt Dorace read the article to us and showed us the other photos on the next page. Mom said we'd already begun teaching others about us. Afterwards, when we'd go back to the mall, folks would recognize us and start talking to my mom.

PLAY TIME

Of course, I don't have to work all the time. I get lots of playtime too. I remember that first day Mom and I played in Zack's Yard. She tried to hide my big red kong in her right hand, but I spotted it. I got so excited! I started swishing my tail and began to whine. The more excited I got, the louder I would whine. Mom just laughed and headed for the back door.

"What's that, Mom? Are we going to play? Oh, boy! I love to play. Come on, Mom. Let's go!"

Zack's Yard is very large with lots of trees and shrubs. I could feel my mom begin to tense up a little as she pondered whether I would return when she called me or if I would run off instead.

"Don't worry, Mom. I'd never leave you."

She began to look around as though she were searching for something. We walked over to the truck and she fished out a long rope from the toolbox.

"What's that for, Mom?"

She took one end and threaded it through a loop in my collar. Once more she looked around, trying to decide where to secure the other end. She seemed very satisfied with her decision as she began looping that rope around her leg. She'd tethered us *together!*

"Okay, Mom! We're really going to play together now."

She took my kong with her right hand, raised it way back behind her body and flung it really hard. That Kong must have traveled 75 feet, but the rope was only 50 foot long.

"Uh, oh!" shouted Mom. "I shouldn't have done that."

I raced towards my kong and Mom came running behind me. I was faster than she was, though. I snatched my kong out of the air just before it plummeted towards the ground. When I whirled around to return my toy to her, Mom was sprawled out on the grass. I'm not exactly sure *how* she got there, but she must have been having fun, though, because she was laughing so hard she could hardly talk.

"Oh, boy! A new game! Let's play 'drag Mom' again."

Aunt Dorace saw the whole thing and zoomed out the back door towards us. When she was satisfied we were both okay and Mom hadn't killed herself, she started laughing too.

Mom removed that rope from her leg and my collar and we must have played out there for at least another hour or so. We still go outside everyday to play but we haven't used that rope since.

MEETING THE FAMILY

Later that day we were inside recuperating from so much excitement when the front doorbell rang.

"Oh, boy! Company! It must be for me!"

I raced Mom and Aunt Dorace to the front door. Mom slipped my leash onto my collar as Aunt Dorace opened the door. Standing outside was a handsome couple waiting patiently to come in and see *me.*

"Who are these folks, Mom?"

I began to prance and whine. I knew they were there to meet *me.* I got "a little too rambunctious", as Mom says, and raised up on my hind legs, all the while whining louder and louder.

"Let me go meet them, Mom. I don't know who they are, but they must like me. Look at them! They're grinning from ear to ear. They can't wait to meet me. Please, Mom let me go meet them."

Mom had other ideas, though, and commanded me to sit down beside her. I didn't like it much. I'd much rather go see this nice couple at the door. Finally I settled down and Uncle Bill and Aunt Sara came inside.

I loved them right off the bat and once Mom released my leash, I raced into the den to get my rope for us to play with.

Uncle Bill loves to play tug of war and we must have pulled each other all over the living room. He's much stronger than Mom and I got quite a work out that day. Every now and then I'd run over to Aunt Sara's chair and smile at her, as she'd rub my head or back.

Aunt Sara and Uncle Bill love dogs. They have a couple at their house. Occasionally we'll go over to visit. They bark a lot, though. I don't bark at all. I just sit there by Mom's feet while they get scolded for being so noisy.

"Hey, Mom, what's up with Fiesty and Spicey? Why do they make so much noise?"

A couple of days after meeting Aunt Sara and Uncle Bill the doorbell rang again. Once more Mom put me on leash and in a downed position beside her.

"Who is it, Aunt Dorace? *Hurry*, please! Someone else has come to see me."

This time I met Mom's sister, Aunt Patsy, and her daughter, Sheryl. They both came in smiling, but I could sense they were a bit frightened or leery of me. I think they were somewhat surprised to see how big and handsome I was.

"Don't worry, Aunt Patsy! I won't hurt you. I just want to get to know you better. That's all. I don't bite. Heck! I don't even bark. I just love to play and I love to be loved. Don't be afraid."

Mom told me about her brothers and sisters that first day we were matched. She said her brothers, Uncle Bill and Uncle

Arnold, loved dogs, but warned that Aunt Patsy wasn't particularly fond of them.

> "What's up with her, Mom? Doesn't she have any pets?
> If she's never had the unconditional love of a dog, like
> me, then she's never really been loved."

Mom was the youngest and the only one of the four with vision problems. She had to be fitted with thick glasses before she could even begin school and her sight worsened as she got older. Her mom died suddenly when she was around fourteen and her dad suffered for years with throat cancer. She'd been left to take care of the household chores and send herself to school. They had very little money so Mom had to work at a downtown department store every afternoon and on Saturdays. She barely made enough to buy her clothes and school supplies, but she never complained or asked anyone for anything. No sir! Not my mom! She just did what she had to do, and went on to graduate from high school with honors. She found a full time job, where she met Aunt Dorace. They quickly became best friends, going everywhere and doing everything together.

Aunt Dorace was a positive influence on mom, always quick to offer encouragement, enthusiasm, moral support and even constructive criticism when necessary. Aunt Dorace and her parents played a significant role during a very critical time in Mom's life. They offered her security, warmth and love-feelings she'd not had since her own mother died.

Together they were the driving forces that enabled my mom to continue her education by attending college at night. They provided Mom with the emotional, spiritual and physical strength she needed to face Life and its many mysteries.

Although Mom had been born with retinitis pigmentosa,

it wasn't diagnosed until she had graduated high school, begun work and had her own apartment. She was nineteen. By that time she was already legally blind. She always knew there had been a problem, but just figured the reason she continually bumped into things was because she was incredibly clumsy. When the doctor revealed his diagnosis he told her that she'd be totally blind within five years, Mom was relieved to finally find out why her vision was so bad, yet frightened at the probability of such a dark future. She tells folks in her sensitivity and awareness classes that she worried about her condition and the probability of going blind for about 45 minutes. Then, she says, she realized that those were things that she had no control over and if God willed them to be, then she'd just have to live with it. Meanwhile, she intends to continue to enjoy her life and follow whatever path He sets before her.

Mom's first taste of independence was forced upon her as a teenager and she was repulsed at the thought of having to impose on someone else for anything. She worked as the Operations Manager at the Medical University of South Carolina until just a year before getting me. Although her sight diminished to the size of pinholes, few of her colleagues ever knew she had vision problems at all. Sometimes she holds me close to her and tells me about how she struggled for so long trying not to be a burden to anyone even though she was barely able to walk across a parking lot safely.

"Poor Mom! I'm so sorry I wasn't there for you back then. You have me now, though, and I'm gonna take really good care of you. I won't let you bump into anything. No, sir! You can depend on me."

THE FARM

We'd been home a couple of weeks when Aunt Dorace loaded Mom and me in the truck and took us on a long, long drive over a big steel bridge and past lots of tall trees. We were going to the *farm*. The *farm*- even the name sounded like fun.

It seemed like a year had passed before we got to the farm. Mom opened the truck door and got out. I was bouncing around, tail wagging, so excited to see this very special place- this fun farm. I jumped out the truck and realized at once that this was indeed a really great place. My nose immediately went into the air as I got a whiff of an unfamiliar odor. It was coming from where those funny looking dogs were playing out in that wide-open field. Mom called them "cows" and I wanted to run and play with them, but Mom wouldn't let me. She walked me over there to see them, but wouldn't let me get too close. They were curious looking creatures with funny things growing out their heads. Mom was afraid they would hurt me, but they merely looked up at me a time or two and just continued grazing on their grass. They made it look so good that I even tried nibbling on it for a while until Mom caught me.

"No!" She said. "That may make you sick."

" Now, come on Mom! How could it be good for those cows and bad for me? Get real! Don't you know I've eaten my share of grass when I was back in the kennels? "

I stopped though, because I wanted to make my mom happy. She reached down, stroked my handsome head with her hand and said,

" Good boy! Good boy! "
"I love you, Mom, but that grass sure tasted pretty good."

SANTA PAWS

Shortly after we returned home from the farm, Aunt Dorace and Mom started bringing down great, big boxes from the attic. They spent an entire day unpacking those boxes and putting all that stuff all over my house. There were candles and rugs and dishes and linens and things to go on the doors. They even brought down a *tree* with *lights* on it! After hanging long socks from the fireplace and shelves, they announced someone was coming soon. " Santa Paws", as Mom called him, would soon be here. I didn't know so much about that.

" Who is this Santa Paws and where is *he* going to sleep? Not in my bed! No, sir. There was hardly enough room in there for Mom after I get in there. What is this fellow going to eat? I sure hoped he didn't like Iams chicken and rice. That's all mine! What is all the hoopla about anyway? This Santa Paws fellow might just be trouble. I'd better watch out for him. "

I tried staying awake that night, but just couldn't hold out past 11pm. The next morning I found strange little presents had grown under that tree Aunt Dorace had put out. Every day after that I found more and more of those little presents. Mom said they were all mine and she even let me sniff one or two of them, but she'd never let me have one. She said we had to wait on that Santa Paws fellow.

Finally one morning Mom got us all out of bed extra early. Santa Paws had finally come!

"Oh, boy! What fun! "

I felt my mom's excitement and ran around the house, going from room to room, knocking over things with my tail. Patches, Sallie and Uuglee just stood there watching me. Every now and then one would bristle up her tail, arch her back and hiss at me.

" Cats! What do they know, anyway?"

Mom gave us each one of those pretty presents from under that tree. Mine smelled so very good-like peanut butter.

"Yum! Yum! My favorite flavor!"

She said that Santa Paws fellow left it for me. I could hardly wait. When I ripped the paper off, I found a brand new nylar bone just for me.

"Say, I think I might be beginning to like this Santa Paws fellow."

CREEKSIDE ADVENT CHRISTIAN CHURCH

That next Sunday Mom announced that we were going to start going to church. I'd been to church lots of times before in Florida with Momma Cheri, but never with my new mom. I tried to tell her she had nothing to worry about, though. I would take good care of her.

Mom and Aunt Dorace got dressed all up in their fancy clothes, brushed me really, really well and we all got in the car for our first trip to church together. They had decided we would start our new lives together in a new church. When we got to Creekside Advent Christian Church, Mom got me out of the back seat and slipped my harness on me. I carefully guided her across the parking lot, through the churchyard and straight up to the door, where I stopped for her. Mom said we should sit in the back, just in case I needed to go outside and in case somebody might not like the idea of a dog in church.

"Oh, Mom! Who wouldn't want *me* around?"

We went inside and headed for the last pew when Pastor Bobby came up to us and introduced himself.

I like Pastor Bobby. He makes my mom's soul feel good. I can feel the warmth right down my leash whenever Pastor Bobby is around.

Pastor Bobby escorted us all closer to the front of the church. Now, I just guide my mom right to that same seat every Sunday. That's "Zack's Spot" now!

We met lots of folks that day. Mom says they're now our church family. I liked all of them and they loved me! Some would even sneak a little pet every now and then.

I always laid down by my mom's feet while Pastor Bobby preached. Occasionally I'd chime in with my own special "amen", but they called it snoring. Pastor Bobby makes a point to talk about me in church every Sunday. I like that.

On Easter Sunday that year, my mom said something very special was about to happen. After the sermon she and I went out to the fellowship hall and Mom put on her swimsuit. I led her back into the sanctuary when Aunt Jean and Aunt Dorace walked up. Mom handed Aunt Dorace my leash and she disappeared behind a big curtain with Uncle Paul and Pastor Bobby.

"Wait a minute! Hold up a second! Where's my mom going? She needs me! It's dark back here and she can't see."

I almost had Aunt Dorace in a full run as we headed around to the other side of the pulpit. I looked and looked, but couldn't find my mom anywhere. I was really getting nervous!

" Hey! Where is she? She needs me to take her places? Who's going to watch out for her? Be careful, Mom!"

Then that big velvet curtain opened up and who do you think was standing right there in the middle of that big pool of water? It was Pastor Bobby and Mom!

"Hey, Mom! What are you doing in there without me? Are you going swimming? Can I swim too? Be careful, Pastor Bobby! I think I need to jump in there with you."

Aunt Dorace held too tightly to my leash though and just stood there laughing one minute and crying the next. Even Aunt Carolyn was there, snapping pictures! She could hardly hold the camera steady for wiping away her tears. Of course, everyone else in the church was crying too. I'm not sure why, though. I wasn't going to let anything happen to my mom.

"Don't worry, Mom. If you start to get into trouble, I'll save you. Aunt Dorace will just have to jump in with me."

When Pastor Bobby dipped Mom's head under the water, I was only a few feet away. I kept inching my way closer, but finally they came out of there. Aunt Dorace rushed me around to be with Mom and I licked and licked and licked her to be sure she was okay. Whew! By the time we got home that day, I was exhausted and had to take a long nap.

AUNT KAREN AND RUTH

One day Mom and Aunt Dorace were watching television when they say this other blind lady talking about a special kind of audible traffic signal. Her name was Karen and she had a pretty little guide dog named Ruth. Mom looked up Aunt Karen's phone number and soon we were meeting her and Ruth at a nearby restaurant. They hit it off immediately. Aunt Karen invited Mom to join the American Council of the Blind and the Dixie Land Guide Dog Users group and that was the beginning of a great friendship. Soon Ruth and I were guiding Aunt Karen and Mom down that same street where that audible traffic light was.

"What fun! Come on, Mom! I'll lead you around that tree limb."

Aunt Karen and Ruth work in the VA hospital just up the street, so they were both familiar with that neighborhood. I'd never been there before.

"Come on, Zack" Ruthie said, "I'll show you."

I followed her and led my mom safely like the pro I am.

COLUMBIA

A couple of weeks later, Aunt Karen called Mom and asked if we could help some folks who were trying to get a new guide dog protection bill passed in our state. Before I knew what was happening, we were in the car and on our way to a big city called Columbia.

It was cold and raining and we couldn't find a parking space anywhere. Aunt Dorace was getting kind of loud and angry, but she finally found a place to park.

" Oh, no, Mom! Not that old raincoat again! I hate wearing that thing."

We rushed to the Senate Building and that's where we met Aunt Angela, Uncle Billy, Aunt Cynthia and Aunt Patsy. They were cool! Uncle Billy had his guide, Jill, and Aunt Cynthia had her guide Grover with them. We all became good friends fast and Mom, Aunt Dorace and I visited Columbia lots of times after that. Each time those men would walk up to my mom, shake her hand and comment on what a pretty boy I was. I'm quite sure the new "Layla's Law" was passed simply because all those guys loved *me* so much!

THE HOSPITAL

Yes, everyone who saw me fell in love with me immediately. All except one particular man who worked in a hospital in Anderson. My Uncle Arnold lives in that area and he got really sick one day. His wife, Aunt Lynne, wasn't sure if he was going to make it. Aunt Dorace, Aunt Patsy, Mom and I decided we needed to be with them so we drove up the next day. I'd heard a lot about Uncle Arnold and Aunt Lynne and I just knew I was going to like them.

Upon our arrival, we went directly to the hospital. Everyone was watching as I flawlessly guided my mom down the long walkway, up those big concrete stairs and through those massive glass doorways. One lady even said she'd never seen a guide dog before. Lots of folks asked if they could pet me, but Mom told them I was working. The nice lady behind the desk told my mom which room Uncle Arnold was in and I swiftly found the elevator for my mom, like she commanded. We got off on the fourth floor, turned right and began our walk down another long hallway, just like the lady instructed. I could hear people gasping and talking as we walked by. We were quite a site, indeed.

" I am such a handsome fellow! Folks can't help but love me."

We turned at the end of the hallway, just like the lady said and when we got to Uncle Arnold's room, the door was closed and there was a note on it. The note was in code so we all went to the nurse's station to find out what it meant. Mom asked a lady about the note and that's when it happened-World War III.

The lady picked up the telephone and started talking with somebody. She held the receiver next to her chin when she told Mom the hospital's attorney said we'd have to leave. She said the hospital had no policy that referenced the use of service animals and she'd have to take that dog (me) out of the building!

"Can you believe it? They wanted me to leave! *Me!* Why me? I was the best looking thing in that hospital and probably the cleanest, too. *They* were telling mom that she'd have to take *me* outside. Uh, oh! Somebody was surely in for it now! "

Mom told her that I was a guide dog, and the lady repeated it to whoever was on the other end of the telephone. The lady just said theirs was an acute care facility and they didn't have any policies that referenced the use of service animals. Mom asked if she could talk with the attorney and was told that he would not be in his office. The lady hung up the phone and Mom just stood there. Her face was beet red and she was so upset she was trembling. But she never raised her voice nor made a scene. Oh, no! Mom advised the lady that her civil rights were being violated by not allowing me in that hospital. The lady just shrugged and began to walk off. Mom stopped her and said she'd leave, but only if the lady would call the local police department and hospital security so they could document what was happening.

"Yeah, Mom!"

The lady picked the phone up again and began talking with someone. By this time a crowd had gathered. She asked Mom if she wanted to talk with the attorney personally. That's when it really got good.

I heard Mom tell the attorney that the Americans with Disabilities Act guaranteed her the right to have her guide dog anywhere the public was invited and for him to deny her access in to see her brother meant he was violating her civil rights. Mom's face became redder and redder. I really thought she was going to have a stroke, so I edged up closer to her. I could feel her calm down as she began to stroke my head. She almost wore a bald spot on me that day. While Mom and the attorney were on the phone, the aides took Uncle Arnold downstairs for tests and we never got to see him that day. Later on, we found out the note on his door was mere to warn the nursing staff that he had conjunctivitis and they needed to wear gloves when they touched him.

On the way home, Mom called the Department of Justice, Health and Human Services, the governor's office, both U.S. Senators and several state senators. She was really mad! As soon as we got back home, Mom began writing lots of letters to lots of people. When she wasn't on the computer, she was on the telephone, talking with someone about what happened. I barely got a chance to play with my kong that first day.

"Come on, Mom! Who wants to go in that old hospital, anyway?"

A couple of weeks later she got a letter of apology from the head of the hospital, but she just wouldn't let it rest. No sir! She wanted that hospital to let Dixieland and GDUI revisit its newly found existing policy regarding guide dogs and make any changes necessary for it to be ADA compliant. She wanted the hospital to train their staff on this new policy and she wanted them to post this new policy in a public place, like the door or lobby. She also asked the hospital to make a generous donation to Southeastern Guide Dog School. In exchange, she promised to contact the Department of Justice and ask them to file her complaint on record, but to suspend any further investigation into the matter. By doing that, the hospital would be relieved of having to pay a huge fine. Mom also reminded them that Aunt Dorace and Aunt Patsy were with her when she was asked to leave the hospital and that, under the "discrimination by association" portion of the title III Civil Rights access law, their rights had been violated too.

A few months later there was an article about me in the Anderson Independent Newspaper. Not long after that, Mom and I were invited to be present at a special luncheon when the hospital unveiled their new service dog policy. Almost a year passed by when Mom got an email from a lady, thanking her for what she'd done regarding getting that hospital's policy changed. The lady told Mom that her grandmother had recently died in that same hospital and, because of what Mom did, she and her guide dog could visit her during her last days. As she read the lady's note, she wiped away tears and reached down and kissed me. Mom said getting that email made her entire ordeal worth all the effort she's spent.

"See what we did, little Sweet Potato!" You're such a good boy!"

"That's nice, Mom. I love you too. Can we go outside and play kong now?"

CAMPING

We'd really been working hard when Aunt Dorace decided we needed to go camping. Camping! I'd never been camping before!

"Oh, boy! Camping, here we come!"

I ran and got my tug rope, my ball on a band, both my kongs
(for the inside and outdoors) and a couple bones. I was ready.

"Hey, Mom, don't forget my food!" "Don't forget my treats!" "Don't forget my carrots!" "Don't forget my blanket!"

We got everything into the camper, got the camper hitched up to the truck and off we went. We were on our way to the beach.

I loved the beach. Momma Cheri and Daddy Lew had taken me to the beach lots of times when I was little. I love to swim and run and chase my flippee flappee. Mom let me play on the beach all day. When we got back to our camper, I was beat. I could barely hold my head up to eat. After I'd busied that night, I couldn't wait for Mom to wipe me down with my baby wipes, "from my nose to my rose to my toes," as she says, and then she put my night shirt on me. I barely remember jumping in bed that night. I was so tired. Camping was very hard work, but lots of fun too. I decided I liked camping.

We stayed there another couple of days and boy, did I have a great time. I got to meet and play with lots of neat people while we were at the beach. I really enjoyed my camping trip to the beach, but I was ready to get back home too. I didn't think Mom and Aunt Dorace would ever get finished unpacking the camper. I don't know why they needed so much junk, anyway.

"Hey, Mom!" "Don't forget my Kongs, my rope, my toys, and my food!"

MADISON AND MORACE

Patches and the other girls didn't get to go camping with us. Patches had been camping lots of times and lots of places, but she needed to stay home 'cuz she was so old. Uugglee and Sallie were old too, but they'd never been camping. They had to stay home and take care of the house. By this time, Aunt Dorace had brought home two more little yellow and white babies-Madison and Morace.

She found Madison at the farm during the winter when she'd gone to check on things. She brought him home with her to keep him from freezing to death. He was just a very tiny little thing then. His eyes were barely opened. Mom kept him in a big crate by her recliner. She fed him with an eyedropper and was always loving on him and me. I didn't like him very much at first. He took too much of my mom's attention. But, after a while, he began to grow on me and I'd give him a quick lick or two when no one was looking. Madison grew to be a big boy soon and he loved to rub up against me. Every time he got close to me, he'd come over and rub his head on mine.

"Sheez! What's up with you?"

Morace came about 6 months later. Aunt Dorace found her at the farm too. I think it's time for Aunt Dorace to quit going to the farm if she's going to keep bringing back kittens.

Morace was a cute little girl. She was an orange tabby, with a white underbelly and feet. She was also just as bad as she was cute. Morace and Madison both really liked rubbing on me, though. I figure they must think we're related.

They were always in trouble. They liked to knock over things and climb the curtains. I thought Aunt Dorace was going to burst a vessel one day when they got in the living room with all her things. That same day she had Mom build a cattery outside for them to live in. We all got along a lot better together after that and Aunt Dorace quit fussing so much.

> "Thank goodness! I don't have to share my bed with those darn cats anymore. Mom takes up enough room ."

THE WALKATHON

We'd been home only a few months when Mom pulled out our suitcases again.

"Hey! Where are we going now? Don't forget my kong. Don't forget my bones. Don't forget my blanket. Don't forget my Iams."

I was getting a little worried until Mom finally pulled out Zack's bag. I watched to make sure she packed everything I needed.

"Hey, I don't need that raincoat. I definitely don't need that jacket and tie. Get the good stuff! Leave that junk home."

The next morning Mom, Aunt Dorace and I hopped in the car and off we went! We were going to Southeastern to walk in their Paws for Independence Walkathon.

"Oh, boy! Maybe I'll see some of my old buddies there."

I was only 4 months old when I walked in my first walkathon. I got tired and my legs didn't want to work too good. Thank goodness a couple of young girls came by with a red wagon and pulled me the rest of the way. I was just a little fellow then. There were lots of people and I remember keeping a close eye on Mama Cheri. I didn't want her to get lost. The next year, I'd grown bigger and much, much stronger. I was able to pull Momma Cheri around that walk with no trouble at all. I was beginning to get a little concerned, though. My new Mom was a lot bigger than Momma Cheri and her eyes were broken. I'd have to be very careful this time. I can't let my new mom get hurt.

Our journey to Palmetto, Florida took two days. We'd been riding about five hours when we stopped at a motel in Jacksonville. Mom had made advance reservations before we left home to avoid any confusion. We checked in with no problems and went straight on to our room. Aunt Dorace was tired from all that driving, so she took a little nap while Mom and I played with my rope. When Aunt Dorace finally woke up I followed her and led Mom to the adjacent restaurant.

There were a few folks eating when we arrived, but they all stopped when they saw me. Everyone in that room was gawking at me as I led my mom to our booth by the wall. Once she was seated, I settled down and under the table by her feet. The nicest young waitress came over and took their orders. A little while later she returned and apologetically told Mom that her Manager said we'd have to move to another area because of me. He wanted us to sit over in the corner in a smoking area because there weren't any other patrons there at that time. Mom just smiled and motioned the waitress to come closer as she whispered,

"Please explain to your Manager that Zack is my guide dog and that the Americans with Disabilities Act guarantees me access into anywhere the public is invited with him. Now, unless he wants to explain to the Department of Justice why we can't remain at this table, I'd suggest he allow us to continue sitting right here."

The embarrassed young lady just smiled understandingly and disappeared behind a big wall. A minute or two later she reappeared with a big grin on her face.

"You all just stay right where you are. You're fine."

Mom and Aunt Dorace thanked her and continued studying the menu. The restaurant didn't have a large print or a Braille menu, so Aunt Dorace had to read the menu to Mom.

They eventually ordered and ate and I was soon guiding my mom to the counter, like she commanded. When we approached the dark haired man at the register, Mom politely extended her hand and introduced herself. She complimented him on the food and the service and thanked him for reconsidering his decision to reseat her.

The surprised man was obviously caught off guard by Mom's affable attitude and appreciation.

"I trust everything was to your satisfaction, then."

Mom reached in her pouch and pulled out our business cards she'd had printed for occasions just like this one.

"The only thing that could have possibly made our eating experience here any better would have been for you to offer a large print or Braille menu."

"You know, that's a great idea! I bet our older customers would appreciate that too. I see them squinting at our menu all the time. Do you know where I can get some large print menus made up?"

Mom gave the newly educated restaurant manger the information he requested and we went on back to our room.

"See there, little Sweet Potato. We're even teaching folks in Florida about the special needs of the blind. See what you did."

"That's good Mom. Now, can we please go play with my kong?"

We left the motel the next morning and were once again on our way to the walkathon. I knew we were at the right place the moment we finally pulled into the parking lot of that big hotel. I lifted my nose and got a whiff of some very familiar smells. There were lots and lots of other guide dogs all over the place. My mom said I was the best, and the most handsome. I love my mom.

We'd gone upstairs for Mom and Aunt Dorace to unpack all their junk and for me to eat dinner. They got all gussied up as though they were going somewhere special.

"Oh, no! Here comes that shedding blade and zoom groom again."

The lobby was kind of dark so I had to be very careful leading Mom to the elevator. When we got in, there were at least 4 other guides in there with us.

"Oh, boy!" I felt as though I were back in training.

We got off the elevator on the first floor and Mom said we were going to a party!

"Great! I love parties! I'll get to see lots of my old pals there. Oh, boy! Maybe someone will drop some good stuff on the floor for me to clean up."

Mom won't give me people food, but if it falls on the floor maybe I can grab it before she'll even know what happened.

" Now, let's see...a room full of blind people with lots and lots of food? Yep, I love parties."

MOMMA CHERI AND DADDY LEW

I guided Mom through the masses of people and we were headed for the door she told me to find. There must have been a thousand people and just as many dogs! I had to be very careful with Mom. My leash told me she was a little nervous being in this crowd. Just as we got to the door, Aunt Dorace whispered something in Mom's ear and Mom told me to find the chair.

I led her directly to that big, high backed chair sitting next to the front door. Then I heard a very familiar voice.

"Could it be? Is it really him?" I twisted my head around all those legs and tried with all my might to find where that voice was coming from. All of a sudden, I saw the top of a gray-haired head coming towards us. As he got closer, I knew exactly who it was.

"Daddy Lew! Daddy Lew! "

Then I heard another familiar voice.

"Momma Cheri! Momma Cheri!"

They'd come all that way just to see me. Of course, they did! After all, I am *Zack*! I am a good boy.

For just a second or two, I forgot about wearing my harness and I began jumping and twisting and squirming to get to them. That was the first time Mom wasn't too upset about me getting distracted. She just smiled and hugged Momma Cheri and Daddy Lew. I wanted to jump up and hug them all too, but I stayed in the downed position. Mom just laughed and understandingly unsnapped my harness to let me play with everyone.

We spent that entire evening together. Mom did something really cool-she handed Daddy Lew my leash and let us spend some "guy time" together.

"Thanks, Mom. I really needed that."

The next day Aunt Dorace, Mom and I met Momma Cheri and Daddy Lew at the walkathon. They'd brought Mikey, Brie and another little guy to walk with us. We started out together, but they really had a hard time trying to keep up with Mom and me. I'd walked that course before, but never as a guide. Momma Cheri and Daddy Lew were amazed each time I'd stop to show Mom the curbs and railroad tracks. They really flipped out when they noticed I was guiding Mom away from the low-hanging limbs and shrubs growing next to the sidewalk. Momma Cheri told Mom that she'd successfully raised 3 guide dogs before but never had a chance to see one in actually work in harness. She and Daddy Lew were so proud of me.

Mom just smiled and said in her special way,

"Good boy! That's my little Sweet Potato! That's my little man!"

I inched over just that much closer to her leg, threw my fluffy tail in the air and began prancing. Just when I thought that day couldn't possibly get any better; the announcer called out Daddy Lew's name. He'd won a cruise!

"Oh, boy! Momma Cheri and Daddy Lew were going on a cruise and it was all because they came down to see *me*."

Mom, Aunt Dorace, Momma Cheri and Daddy Lew were sitting around talking and laughing and eating. Mikey, Brie, and I were snoozing under the table when I suddenly got the urge to go. I got up and nudged Mom's hand with my nose, looked at her with my beautiful brown eyes and cocked my head that special way to tell her I needed to busy. Just as she started to stand, she did something really neat. She handed Daddy-Lew my leash and asked if he'd take me to the relief area. She knew he wanted to spend some more "man" time with me.

"Thanks, Mom. We won't be long. I won't go far. Now, you sit right there and don't you move. I'll be right back and get you. Don't worry, Mom. I'll come back and get you."

That evening Momma Cheri and Daddy Lew came back and joined us for dinner. Afterwards we all went back upstairs to our suite so I could play with all my neat new toys they'd brought me. Then Aunt Kathleen came over with her guide, Maya. Mom and Aunt Kathleen took our leashes off and let us run and jump and play until we were both so tired, we just dropped on the floor.

"Can you believe it? Me on the floor?"

At that particular moment in time, I really wouldn't have cared if it didn't even have carpet on it. It had been a very long, busy day and I was exhausted. I barely remember saying good-bye to Momma Cheri and Daddy Lew. In fact, I slept through the entire trip home, except the few times we stopped for me to busy. We'd traveled quite a distance that weekend and did lots of fun things. Mom was so happy. She said we'd raised enough money to sponsor another guide dog puppy, just like me, 'cept she'd asked for a little girl. She was going to name her, "Dorace" in honor of Aunt Dorace. Mom said Aunt Dorace had been her sighted guide for so many years and she loved me so much that it was only right to name a guide dog after her.

"What do you think, little Sweet Potato?"

Mom asked as she held me close to her.

I just gave her my special lick of approval and wagged my fluffy tail.

"Okay, Mom, but why a *little girl?*"

BLESSING OF THE GUIDES

I like girls, okay, but everyone knows boys are the best. Of course, I can't say that in front of Ruth or Lunar or Maggie. They may take exception to that.

I met Maggie and Aunt Carmella when Aunt Dorace took Aunt Karen, Ruth, Mom and me to Columbia for a Dixieland Guide Dog Users meeting. We all went into the beautiful Green Street Methodist Church and the pastor gave a special "Blessing of the Dogs." Mom dressed me in my gold jacket and black tie and Aunt Dorace took lots and lots of pictures. Everyone told how their guides had changed their lives. Mom gently stroked my head as she remembered God revealing His purpose for her life the first day she was at Southeastern. She knew He wanted her to be an advocate for the blind and he continued to open the doors to allow her the opportunity to do just that. Mom said that, in a way, *I* led her to God.

"Uh, oh! Grab the tissues! Aunt Dorace is crying again."

After our meeting, we all walked the 8 blocks to the capital building. You should have seen us-Ruth, Maggie, Jill, Speedo and me as we led our moms and dads around that big old building and across the Capital grounds. We got lots of attention from everyone passing by. I knew they were all looking at *me*. I raised my fluffy tail and began prancing as I safely guided my Mom back to the church. We'd gotten lots of exercise on our trip that day, so Ruth and I slept all the way back home. I like being with Mom and Aunt Dorace, but I really like it when there's another guide around-especially a beautiful lady like Ruth.

PUPPY RAISERS

As the days got longer, Mom found more for us to do.

"Gee whiz, Mom. Blind folks aren't supposed to be so active. Don't you know that?"

People were always asking Mom to come talk about *me*. We must have gone to a hundred businesses; hospitals, organizations and groups as Mom delivered Sensitivity and Awareness classes to their members. The more we did; the more they'd ask us to do. They still call almost everyday, asking us to come and tell them about guide dogs the special needs of the blind. Mom says it's our responsibility to give back to the community. She says God wants us to teach them.

The next week we rode down to Bluffton to meet some prison inmates who were also puppy raisers for Southeastern Guide Dog School. I had a great time that day, showing all those guys how a professional guide works. They have to stay locked up in that building and rarely get a chance to personally see a finished guide team. They were dazzled by my good looks and astounded by my work.

"Shoot! You ain't seen nothing yet!"

We spent the entire morning with those guys and we all hugged each other before we left. When they started telling how they'd each ended up in prison, Mom stopped them.

"What you did in a previous life was just that- a previous life. That's over and done with. It's what you're doing now that's so important. I have a little sight left and I can't see those stripes you're wearing for the wings sprouting from your shoulders and the halos from your heads."

A few weeks later we saw some of those same guys on television. They were on a program called "Cell Dogs" on the Animal Planet channel.

Mom loved puppy raisers and always went out of her way to thank them for the love, care, attention, and devotion they spend on their puppies. I remember the day before the walk-athon we met a couple of puppy raisers from Texas-Aunt Teresa and Uncle Don. They were returning their little guy, Willie, back to the school for professional training and had stopped in the Cracker Barrel for lunch. Mom said God orchestrated that meeting because we were in a restaurant miles away from where we should have been hours after we should have eaten when they walked in.

Mom suddenly got up and said,

"Forward, Zack! Find the wall!"

Somehow I just knew where she wanted to go, so I led her around all those people and tables and chairs like the pro that I am. I didn't even stop for the first sniff. As we approached, Uncle Don scooted over to the next chair and told Mom to sit down.

"I don't know if I can complete this conversation without crying, " she confessed. "I don't even know exactly why I'm here. I just know I felt compelled to come over and thank you for what you're doing."

"That's okay," Don replied. "We've cried this entire weekend. We appreciate your joining us. As your guide led you through this darkened, crowded room I realized the importance of what we're doing and how difficult it would have been for you without him."

Uncle Don looked lovingly at me as Mom began to tell him all about me.

Their little boy, Willie, was under their table, proudly wearing his blue training jacket. They'd had him since he was 8 weeks old and kept him almost a year. Now, it was time to give him up and pick up another.

We saw Uncle Don and Aunt Teresa several times that weekend. They were sad after the walk, as they were headed to the school, where they dropped off their precious little boy. That night at the pizza party, though, their tears had turned into laughter as they handed Mom their new fluffy bundle, Cassius.

"Hey, watch it there, little fellow! That's my mom! Don't get too close!"

VACATION

With all those sensitivity and awareness engagements we were going to, I was getting a little frazzled. Then Mom said we were going to Disney World on vacation!

"Okay, Mom! I get a vacation! I'm going to Disney World! Don't forget my kong! Don't forget my toys! Don't forget my bones! Don't forget my Iams Grab Zack's Bag and let's go! Whoa, Mom! You're taking the whole container of Iams! Well, all right! That's what I'm talking about! Let's go! We're off to Disney World!"

But that wasn't our first and only stop. Oh, no! When Aunt Dorace takes a vacation, she *really* takes a vacation! We stayed a couple of days in a neat place next to the ocean at Daytona Beach. Aunt Kathleen, her guide, Maya; Uncle Vaughn, his guide, Marcelle, and their friends Uncle Glenn and Aunt Bonnie came over and visited for a while. Marcelle, Maya and I got a chance to run and play while the big guys sat around and talked. Marcelle and I really liked to play with my tug rope. We took turns pulling each other around the rooms. Maya wasn't too interested in playing with us guys. She just wanted to sit next to her mom. After a while, though, I got bored with it, too, so I went over and rested my head on Mom's leg. She gave me a big kiss on my muzzle and said,

"That's my little Sweet Potato! That's my little man."

"I love you, too, Mom."

Later we went to a cool Doggy Park not far from Aunt Kathleen's house. Maya just walked around and sniffed everything. Mom brought my flippee flappie and we must have played for an hour. She'd throw it and I'd go get it and take it back to her. Sometimes I would even catch it in mid air. Mom sings to me when we play. She makes up special songs just for me.

"Zack, Zack, get the toy and bring it back!" Or she may sing, "Hey! Hey! Whaddaya say? Look at my little boy play!"

She sings to me all the time, even when she takes me to busy. I like it when Mom sings a special song just for me. When we're in public, though, folks look at Mom kind of weird-like; but she doesn't care. She ignores them and just keeps on singing.

"I really do love you, Mom."

After a couple of days at Daytona Beach, we finally re-loaded the car and headed for Disney World!

"Okay, now that's what I'm talking about! Vacation at last!"

I could hardly wait.

DISNEY WORLD

It was a very short trip from Daytona Beach to the Disney All-Star Sports Resort. When we got there I jumped right out that car and led Mom straight to the registration desk.

"Look out, ya'll! Big blind lady coming through! Please step out the way."

Right away I figured out that resort didn't have too many of us working guys staying there. It seemed like everyone there tried to reach down and pet me.

"Hey, guys! Can't you see I'm trying to work here? I don't have time to stop and play. I've got to guide my mom to our room."

We must have made a hundred trips to unload the car. I've never seen so much luggage! Mom and Aunt Dorace even brought a little refrigerator they bought especially for our trip. When I saw them pull that microwave out the trunk, I really did flip out.

"Wow, Mom! We've got an entire kitchen in here. Now, when does *my* vacation begin?"

We rested a little while after unpacking everything. I was glad. It was a long way from our room to the car.

"Now, let's see. Which one of these beds is ours, Mom?"

Mom carefully removed the pretty, brightly decorated resort bedspread and replaced it with one she'd brought from home.

"We need to always be considerate of others and their property."

Mom folded the spread neatly and gently placed it on the top shelf of the closet. I got a couple of quick winks, ate my dinner and Mom took me outside to busy

"Geeze, where did all these people come from?"

There must have been thousands of them out there playing on that football field right in front of our room. I liked being able to just lay there and watch them. I wasn't wearing my harness so every now and then Mom would let me pet one. She always held tight to my leash though. I decided I liked this vacation stuff pretty good until Aunt Dorace announced we were going to the Magic Kingdom. Mom harnessed me up and told me she needed me to take her to the bus stop.

"Sure, Mom. How difficult could that be? Let's go."

We just had to walk back down to the pool; turn right; go through the big doors, down the long lobby and through 2 more big doors. Then we'd be at the bus stop

"Come on, Aunt Dorace. Let's go see Mickey, Minnie, Goofy and my personal favorite, Pluto!"

We only had to wait a short while until the bus arrived. Folks there were really nice and let Mom and me board the bus first. Mom always wrapped both legs around me to protect my paws. She was so afraid someone would step on me. Away we went to the Magic Kingdom!

When we got off the bus we had to walk a long, long way until we finally got to the main entrance of the Magic Kingdom. Once we gave them our tickets, we went straight to Guest Services for a special identification card and to find out where my relief areas were. Boy! Was that ever an experience! Their instruction booklet says to ask a cast member. Most didn't even know that they were cast members, not to mention what a relief area was. One lady directed Mom to the *Ladies'* room.

"I guess she must think I *really* am smart, eh, Mom? Tee Hee."

Frustrated, Aunt Dorace told Mom to just "come on" and that we'd "wing it" when the time came. I love Aunt Dorace. Mom doesn't want to hurt anyone's feelings and always takes time to explain things so nicely to everyone, even if they don't care. Aunt Dorace wants to get things done; get them done her way and on *her* schedule. If feelings get hurt, that's just too bad.

We walked across Main Street and up the stairway to the train station, where we caught the locomotive to "Adventure Land." So far, I was enjoying my vacation. We got off the train and headed towards a big bridge with gazillions of people on it. They all seemed to be staring at a huge ride speeding straight down Thunder Mountain.

"Mom! We aren't going on that thing, are we? I-I'm not afraid for myself, but M-Mom, I just don't think you're up to riding that thing. We, I mean You could get hurt."

Thankfully we continued on past the throngs of people and went in to see some funny bears sing and play musical instruments. From there we walked over to the "Hall of Presidents", then to the "Haunted Mansion." It's a Small World was next; then, on to see the Tiki Bird Show. The folks at Walt Disney World always treated us really special and seated my mom in a safe place. Of course, I was constantly right by her side, safely guiding her everywhere.

It was dark when we finally got ready to leave the Magic Kingdom. I was quite sure I was going to have to lead Mom and *carry* Aunt Dorace back to the bus stop. Everyone was quiet on our ride back to the resort. When we got off the bus, I guided Mom through the big doors; down the long lobby; through the other big doors; left at the pool; down the walkway to the complex; and then, to our room. We'd been there about 10 minutes when Aunt Dorace called Mom on the walkie-talkies. She couldn't keep up with Mom and me and was not able to find her way back to our room. So Mom put her shoes back on, harnessed me up and off we went to get Aunt Dorace. I thought that was soooo funny. Mom can see just a little in the daylight; but she's totally blind at night. Aunt Dorace, however, can see a speck on a gnat! Yet, off we went to find Aunt Dorace and show her the way back to our room!

We spent an entire week at Disney World. We visited every theme park and saw lots and lots of things. I didn't care too much for those Disney characters, though. I tried to keep Mom as far away from them as possible. When we went to Africa at the Animal Kingdom, I especially didn't like those natives wearing strange-looking headdresses. Mom wanted to get closer, but I'd much rather stay away from them, thank you.

The nice man sat us in a very special spot to see "the Lion King". When the dancers came out, they couldn't keep their eyes off me. They could obviously appreciate things of beauty. We walked and walked and walked all over the Animal Kingdom. When we finally got back to our room, we all just dropped!

"Whew! It's good to get off my little feet!"

I think my favorite spot in all of Disney World was at Fort Wilderness. We rode over to the campground on a cool ferry launch from the Magic Kingdom. Mom and Aunt Dorace ate a huge lunch at the Trails End restaurant and then we walked around the petting zoo. The animals there seemed quite surprised to see a handsome working man like me, but they were very nice. It was great being around creatures more like me for a while.

Folks at Disney World were quite nice to us while we were there. They had a hard time understanding that my mom's eyes were broken, though. When she'd ask for directions, they'd invariably point or use a color-descriptive landmark.

"Duh! Why do you think my mom has me? Can't you just offer to have us follow you to where ever she wants to go? Mom can't see where you are pointing and she definitely won't be able to recognize a blue pole.'

VISITING SOUTHEASTERN

Our week at Disney World ended much too soon and we were suddenly back in the car. Instead of heading east, though, we were going west.

"Mom, we're going the wrong way! Oh, no. We're lost again."

After a week of *them* getting lost and *me* having to find our way back to our motel room I was much too exhausted to care. My mom was sitting in the front seat. She wasn't walking any-where, and if she needed me, I was right there.

"Think I'll just settle down for a nice long nap."

We hadn't been traveling very long at all when Aunt Dorace slowed the car down. We made a sharp left turn and then an-other. I found enough energy to raise up off my back seat when I got a glimpse of something very familiar.

"Can it really be? Yep! "

I recognized the big building located just in front of us. There, to the left were the kennels where I lived while in train-ing. Just beyond that were the puppy kennels where I was born. We were back at Southeastern.

"Zackie, we're going back in to see everyone. Don't

you worry, Sweet Potato. Mom's not going to leave you there. Oh, no! You're Momma's little man. You're part of me. I can't leave you."

I wagged my tail and could hardly wait to get harnessed up and go see Aunt Helen and Aunt Sue and Uncle Jim and Aunt Heidi and Uncle Aaron.

Everyone was so glad to see me. They all said I was "the perfect guide dog."

"Of course, I am! You should have already known that."

We stayed and talked with everyone for a couple of hours or so. It was so good to see them again, but it was getting time for my dinner.

"Okay, Mom. Let's wrap it up! I'm getting hungry and I haven't even begun to play yet."

We left the school and rode down to a near-by motel, just off I-75 in Bradenton. Aunt Dorace went in the office to register while Mom put my harness on me and we just walked around to stretch our legs a little.

"Geez, Mom! After a week at Disney World, my legs are stretched all the way to South America!"

Aunt Dorace finally came out and told Mom our room number. Now Mom has a little usable vision and had already noticed that all the rooms on one side of the motel had even numbers. When Aunt Dorace told us we were staying in room

31, Mom told her it must be on the opposite side of the hotel. We walked over there while Aunt Dorace drove the car. A man came up and said something to Aunt Dorace and she disappeared into the office again. She came out and told Mom that she needed our identification.

"Uh, oh! Someone is in trouble now."

It seems as though the owners of the hotel were from a foreign country and were not familiar with our laws. When they first found out I was traveling with my mom and Aunt Dorace, they said we couldn't stay because of health department regulations. Then they said we'd have to pay an extra clean up fee. Then they said my mom didn't "look blind" and wanted proof that she was.

Mom confronted the folks in the office. The lady owner spoke with a heavy accent and called in her husband, who also had a heavy accent.

"You're not blind," he shouted. "I watched you and you could see the numbers on the door. You knew where the room was. You're not blind. Why do you need that dog? Prove you are blind."

Mom just told the man that he could not, by law, ask for any documentation, once she'd identified me as a service animal and that she most definitely did not have to prove anything to him.

"Okay, Mister, you're in for it now! Mom's face is turning red. You're in big trouble."

The loud man kept yelling at my mom. There were lots of people in the lobby, but they all said the man was crazy, so they left.

Mom just looked the irate man right square in his eyes, laughed and said,

"Call your lawyer. I know you have one, so just call him. Tell him everything you've said to me and everything you've asked for from me. Maybe he can tell you what kind of trouble you are already in."

The man realized Mom was serious and he did call someone. A short time later he came over and apologized. Mom gave him our card and a card from Southeastern Guide Dog School.

"Call these people and ask them to help you establish a policy that references the use of service animals-particularly guide dogs. Ask them to help train you and your staff on the Americans with Disabilities Act that references access issues and civil rights. Make a donation to Southeastern for their troubles and put a decal on your front door that says, 'Service Animals Welcomed, '" she said. "I'll file a complaint with the DOJ and ask them to suspend an investigation. That way you won't be charged a possible $50,000 fine. I'll check back later to be sure you've complied."

We ended up spending the night there, but left the next day. I didn't even get a chance to play with my kong. But it didn't matter. We were going to see Aunt Millie.

AUNT MILLIE

We met Aunt Millie last year when Mom and I were matched. She was lots of fun and seemed to always know what to say to make my mom feel better. A few times I could sense Mom was getting a little sad or homesick, even with me right there licking her face. We'd walk down to the living room and find Aunt Millie. Soon Mom would be laughing again and I'd be chasing flying drink bottles.

"Oops! I wasn't 'spose to say anything 'bout that."

After getting lost a couple of times, Mom telephoned Aunt Millie and she met us at a gas station. We followed her to her house and we sat around about an hour or so laughing and talking. Well, they were; I just wagged my tail mostly and kept a sharp lookout for any bottle that might go flying across the room.

Aunt Dorace wanted to go to the beach, so we all piled in Aunt Millie's Tracker and away we went. Aunt Millie took the top off because Mom asked her to. That was really cool! Aunt Millie drove and Mom and I sat in the front passenger seat. Aunt Dorace and Aunt Toni somehow squeezed themselves in the back. It's a real good thing the beach wasn't too far away, though. I'm not so sure that little car could have taken much more of us.

When we got to the beach Aunt Dorace and Aunt Millie jumped in the water. I wanted to go too, but I could feel how scared my mom was to let me.

"Geez, Mom! I've got on my nylon collar and leash. I know how to swim. What's the big deal? Come on, Mom. Let me go swimming."

At last Mom took me to the edge of the water so we could wade.

"Yeah, right. I want to go out there with Aunt Dorace!"

Soon Aunt Dorace came over and took my leash and walked me out until I could swim. I could swim!

"Look, Mom! I told you I could swim. Don't worry! You just stay right there and don't move. I'll be back after I swim around just a little while longer."

Boy! What a great time we had at the beach! I knew I loved Aunt Millie. She took me swimming at the beach. Much too soon we were all soaking wet and packed in that little Tracker, headed back to Aunt Millie's house. After Mom washed the salt water off me and dried me, we were in Aunt Dorace's car and headed for Sarasota.

ZACK'S SPECIAL SURPRISE

Mom and Aunt Dorace registered at this motel without incident and we went to our room and unpacked. Well, they unpacked. I was too tired to do much of anything at that moment. I just wanted to sleep.

"Be careful, Mom. Remember, I'm not wearing my harness and you're on your own."

I woke up from my short nap and Mom was on the phone.

"Who's she talking with? She doesn't know anyone here."

"Zackie, Mom's got a big surprise for you but you have to go busy first."

"What's she talking about? Surprise? All right! I love surprises. Let's go!"

I guided Mom over to a grassy area and stopped at every step, even without my harness on.

"Shoot! I don't really need that thing to work. It's mostly to show folks I'm a guide dog anyway. "

I wanted to hurry back and get my surprise.

"I wonder what it could be?"

When we got back to our room a car drove up.

"Here they are," said Aunt Dorace.

"Here who are?" I wondered. "Will they keep me from getting my surprise? I hope not."

I looked up to see who was getting out of the little station wagon that parked next to us

"I hope they don't stay long. I want my surprise."

Then, I immediately recognized that soft voice say,

"Zack! Hi, there, Zack"

It was Momma Cheri and Daddy Lew! They were my surprise!

"Oh, thank you, Mom! Thank you! Thank you! Thank you."

We all got in that station wagon and started out to show my mom where I used to live. I watched carefully as we drove through the gates and up the driveway. As soon as we got out the car I recognized Mikey and Brie when they called to me.

"But who is *this* little fellow and what is *he* doing here?"

"That's Ashe!" Momma Cheri explained. "We sponsored Ashe and are his puppy raisers. He's only 8 months old, so be careful with him, Zack."

Mom was a little nervous at first, but Momma Cheri and Daddy Lew assured her I'd be okay.

"Heck, Mom! I grew up here. I know every little tree and have probably watered every little blade of grass out here. I'll be okay."

Mikey was so glad to see me. He, Ashe and I jumped and ran and played and swam all evening. Brie just wanted to make sure that I remembered that she was and still is boss of this household.

"Okay, Big Sis. I get it. I just want to spend a little time with you guys again. That's all."

The time flew by and we soon found ourselves back in that little car. This time Mikey, Brie and Ashe were in there with us. At Aunt Dorace's suggestion, we stopped by to see Momma Cheri's mom and dad. I loved them so much. They kept me when I was little sometimes when Momma Cheri and Daddy Lew needed to go out somewhere without me. Grandpop still carried treats around in his pocket for us and Grandmom was still as sweet and loving as always. They loved seeing me and I really loved seeing them too.

"Thanks for the treat, Grandpop."

When we got back to the motel Momma Cheri and Daddy Lew left with Brie, Mikey and Ashe. It had been so good to spend some time with them again. I was sad to have to say good bye.

"So long, you guys. Take real good care of Momma Cheri and Daddy Lew. I love all you guys, but I love my new Mom too and she really needs me. I'm a working man now, you know. I've got a job to do."

The next day we packed up the car and headed home.

"Oh, boy! Home! So this is what a vacation is like? Well, I had no idea I'd be so pooped."

It was going to be so good to get back to my house with my things, especially *my* bed! Oh, I let Mom sleep in there with me, but it's really mine.

WHITE CANE DAY

We hadn't even gotten all our things unpacked good when Mom had yet another project for us. We were going to host Charleston's "White Cane Day" and the mayor and lots of other folks were going to be there.

"Uh, oh! Here comes that darned shedding blade and zoom groom again."

I must have guided Mom to a hundred meetings and our phone rang constantly. Finally, the big day arrived. Aunt Dorace drove us down to the Visitors' Center, where dozens of folks were already waiting. I don't know why, but this was the first "White Cane Awareness Day" ever in Charleston and blind people came out from the woodworks.

We all met at the downtown Visitors' Information Center. Aunt Karen and Ruth were there with some of the local blind veterans. Aunt Nancy was there with Luna and another nice lady with a strange name-Tweety. I liked Aunt Tweety immediately and she really liked me too. She told my mom she wanted a guide dog just like *me*!

"Thanks, Aunt Tweety. Once you get your guide, you'll be able to throw that old white cane down. You won't need it anymore."

Even Uncle Richard was there with his "certified seeing-eye

person", Tim. Uncle Richard had been helping Mom coordinate the event and, once he met me, he, too, wanted his own guide dog. He was a bit concerned about qualifying, though, because he is in a wheel chair.

"Shoot, Uncle Richard! Those folks at Southeastern can train one of my buddies to guide you, even if you are in that chair They trained Tiger to guide Aunt Patti and she was in a motorized wheel chair."

Pastor Bobby and Aunt Susan; Mayor Riley and Brianna and Mom and I led the parade of blind walkers down Meeting Street the 4 blocks to Francis Marion Square. Aunt Gwynnette and Uncle Richard had set up a bandstand, a couple of tents and lots of chairs. Ryan's Steak House even sent their mascot and they generously donated some delicious cookies, tea, and cold water. The local visually impaired school kids were there too. Everything got really quiet when the United States Air Force Honor Guard marched up to "fly the colors." Just at that very moment, little Shelby, a blind 7-year-old, began to sing the National Anthem. When Shane, a very talented college student, finished his song, "Don't Laugh at Me," there wasn't a dry eye around. I even had a tear or two in my eyes. The mayor was quite pleased with everything and asked Mom to please make this an annual event.

"Yeah, Mom! Way to go!"

COMMUNITY AWARENESS

A week or so after the "White Cane" celebration Mom and I participated in a "No See'um" golf tournament with some local visually impaired veterans. I rode on the neat golf carts and wanted to go chase those silly little balls, but Mom wouldn't let me. After a while, I got bored and just stayed on the cart. I watched as Uncle Charlie and Aunt Jackie took good care of my mom, though.

After the golf tournament it seems we had something to do every day. We went to a couple of conventions; one, in Myrtle Beach. A few days later we went back to Columbia for another Dixieland meeting. That's when Mom was elected President. I was so proud of her. I had no idea what all that entailed; but I was still proud of her. She was President because of *me!*

RILEY

A week or so later, Mom got a very upsetting email about an abandoned guide dog right here in North Charleston.

"What? How could someone abandon one of us? We're part of them. We're their eyes! It must be a mistake."

It was no mistake, though. A blind lady left her guide of 9 years at the vet's office, with instructions to "put her down." I wasn't sure what that meant, but it couldn't be good.

Mom found out the guide had come from a school up north and contacted their local representative. They said they'd be glad to ship the guide dog back up there, but it would be better for the dog if we could find a home locally for her. Mom asked Aunt Dorace if there was anything we could do and the next thing I knew we were speeding to that vet's office to rescue Riley.

When we got there, the vet went over everything again with Mom and Aunt Dorace. She told how she'd donated her services for Riley for years and how Riley's handler just left her there. It seems she was concerned over some health issues Riley had and would rather "put her down" than deal with them.

"Let me go get her," the vet said. "Then you can decide for yourself."

We heard the scuffle of some feet coming down the hallway and just then, the door to the examining room we were waiting in flew open. In stepped a huge, yellow lab, just like me. She must have weighed a hundred pounds or more! She was still wet from the bath the technician had given her.

"Her first bath in years, I think, " confessed the tech.

Riley was obviously quite fat and quite old; but, yet, she was also quite regal too. She quickly scoped out that examining room and assessed the situation. She walked straight up to Aunt Dorace, constantly shaking that big furry tail, and gently laid her big head in Aunt Dorace's lap.

"Uh, oh! That did it! Looks like we're going to have one more at our house!"

When we got back home I took out all my toys and showed them to Riley. That really took a long time, too. Riley just laid there as I showed her my rope and my kong and my ball and my bone. She never moved from Aunt Dorace's side.

"Silly girl! Don't you know what a toy is? Don't you know how to play?"

Mom warned me that Riley was really old and couldn't play like I do.

"Maybe not, Mom. But she can sure *eat* as much as I do though. Hey. Mom! That's my Iams! Can't she get her own?"

Now that we have Riley, she goes everywhere Aunt Dorace goes. Sometimes they even leave Mom and me at home while they make trips to the store or the farm.

"Watch out for those funny looking cows, Riley, and please, please don't let Aunt Dorace bring back any more of those darn kittens."

Riley has even taken several trips with us, but Mom always makes sure we stay in a "pet friendly" hotel. Since Riley is retired now, she is no longer a service animal but a pet. Aunt Dorace says she's a very "special" pet, though.

One day a lady from the national organization, Guide Dog Users, Inc., phoned my mom and asked her to write a story about Riley. She did and that story was included in their newsletter, *"Paw tracks."* Later we learned that story was nominated for a special award. Mom was surprised and very happy. She kissed Riley and me. I was excited too. I licked Mom and even kissed Riley.

"Ugh!"

I forgot I was still upset with her for hiding my kong.

We'd been playing earlier that day. Mom would throw my kong and I'd go get it. Sometimes I'd even catch it in mid air. Everything was going just fine and we were having lots of fun until Mom got up and walked over to the fence. Now, even though I was "off harness", I still couldn't let my mom get hurt; so I left my kong and ran over to check out what my mom was doing. When I went back to where I'd left my kong, it was gone!

"Quick, Mom! Call the police! Someone's stolen my kong!"

We looked and looked, but couldn't find my kong anywhere. Riley didn't seem to be the least bit interested and just laid there, stretched out in the sunshine. Mom finally gave up and said she'd find it whenever she cut the grass.

"What? That's *my* kong? I can't wait until then."

Mom insisted we go back inside, though, so Riley stood up and that's when I spotted it-my kong! Riley had been laying on it all that time.

AUNT CAROLYN

Aunt Carolyn gave me my first kong when she, Aunt Dorace and I brought Mom home from Southeastern. She has lots of dogs and cats at her house and sometimes comes over to take care of ours when we go out of town. Every time she comes over for a visit, she always grabs my head and tells me how handsome I am. Aunt Carolyn knows a lot about animals, especially service dogs. She suggested my mom should have a guide dog a long, long time ago. Thank goodness Mom finally listened to her! I guess, in a way, Aunt Carolyn is responsible for my mom getting me.

"I love Aunt Carolyn!"

She loves me too. I remember once, when we went to Myrtle Beach to help with a "Low Vision Fair," Aunt Dorace got hungry, so we went to a big restaurant for lunch. After they ate, we all got up and approached the cash register. There must have been a hundred people standing there! Aunt Carolyn and Mom decided to wait outside while Aunt Dorace stayed to pay the bill.

"Forward, around, Zack," Mom commanded.

Away we went! I guided my mom around *all* those folks. Some were standing in pairs, blocking the narrow hall, so I just led Mom right through them. Aunt Carolyn was amazed and had to rush to keep up with us. She was used to my mom standing politely, waiting for folks to move or get out of her way. She definitely was not prepared to see my mom negotiate that big crowd so quickly. She still talks about that day.

BEING A TOURIST

After our long vacation in Disney World, going to a couple of meetings in Myrtle Beach and Columbia, and adopting Riley, Mom and Aunt Dorace decided we should stay home a while.

"Thank goodness! Now, maybe a guide can rest a while."

The next thing I knew, Aunt Dorace was going back upstairs bringing out those big boxes and that huge tree again. My mom ordered Riley and me a great big inflatable, illuminated Santa and Reindeer to go outside. I loved to watch it "wake up" each night, but Riley would just bark.

I was already getting excited about that Santa Paws fellow leaving me another nylar bone.

"Can I please have a chicken flavored one this time?"

Christmas came and I did get my bone, along with a lot of other neat things. Mom and Aunt Dorace repacked all the Christmas decorations and put them away. I don't know how they got those great big yard ornaments back in their little, tiny boxes.

A week or so later Aunt Dorace told Mom to get us ready to "be a tourist in our hometown." Each year the City of Charleston offers its residents a ticket that will allow them entrance into 20 local attractions for a very special price. Aunt Dorace and Mom had given each other one of those tickets for Christmas.

"Oh, boy! I get to show my mom the city."

I loved going downtown! I especially liked seeing all those funny-looking fish at the new Aquarium. Mom always tells me to take her next to that big fish tank, where we watch the divers at feeding time.

"I wonder if their food tastes as good as mine?"

Mom almost brushed my coat off, like she always does when she gets me ready to go somewhere.

"Okay, Mom, I just had my bath yesterday, you know."

At last she put that darn shedding blade down, we got in the car and were headed to downtown Charleston.

Our first stop was the Joseph Manigault House.

When the lady there saw me with my mom, she gave us a special tour. Mom really enjoyed being able to take her hands and feel the antique furnishings, woodworking and decorations in that great big house. The nice lady really took lots of time with Mom and me and that made Mom very happy. Of course, if Mom is happy, I am too.

We visited a couple of more historical homes that day, but I think most of the other folks paid more attention to me than the houses! Some would even try to reach out and pet me.

"Hey, mister! I gotta watch out for my mom! It's really dark in here and she can't see too well. She needs me to guide her around, you know! If you pet me I could get distracted and forget to stop at that step, causing her to fall. I don't want my mom to fall. She's too big and if she falls she could get hurt and she could hurt me too. Can't you read that sign on my harness? It says, 'Please Don't Pet Me-I'm Working.'"

By the end of January, we'd seen Charles Towne Landing, Mepkin Abbey, the Francis Beidler Forrest, Middleton Place, Magnolia Gardens, Drayton Hall, James Island County Park, Old Santee Canal Park and a couple of other downtown mansions. For a blind lady, Mom could surely get around, thanks to me and Aunt Dorace. It seemed like we had somewhere to go everyday.

AUNT LYNNE AND UNCLE ARNOLD

Things settled down for a little while before Mom pulled out Zack's bag.

"Where are we going now, Mom? Don't forget my kong. Don't forget my bones. Don't forget my Iams. Oh, you can leave that raincoat and my jacket home!"

Mom put Riley and me in the backseat and she and Aunt Dorace were in the front. Off we went, again! We were going to see Uncle Arnold and Aunt Lynne and then on a tour of Ivy Creek.

The folks at the Anderson La Quinta were really nice. They loved Riley and me and were amazed that Mom cleans up after us. They said they had lots of sighted guests who wouldn't even think of picking up after their dogs. Mom just smiled and told her that she loved me and it was her responsibility to me and the public to pick up what I put down.

We arrived at Uncle Arnold's house early the next morning. When we got there, even though Mom didn't put my harness on me, I guided her straight to the front door anyway. I stopped to show her the steps when Aunt Lynne opened the door.

I immediately sensed Aunt Lynne really liked animals and I loved her right off the bat. She kept rubbing on Riley and me and telling me what a pretty boy I was. Uncle Arnold had been sick, but he rubbed on me too. He kept talking about how clean and soft we were.

"Of course! You'd be too if someone were brushing on you with a shedding blade all the time."

Then Mom did something she'd *never* done before. She unsnapped my leash! That's right-*my leash*! Aunt Lynne had been begging her to let me play so Mom just reached down and unsnapped my leash!

"Thanks, Mom! I'll be careful. I won't break anything. I promise. Aunt Lynne wants me to play ball with her. Don't worry. You just sit right there! I won't go out of this big room. Hmm. What's all this stuff? Aunt Lynne and Uncle Arnold must have a dog. I've just found all his toys. Oh, boy! What shall we play with first?"

We stayed with them a couple of hours and I was exhausted when we left. That Aunt Lynne sure can wear a little fellow like me out.

"Whew! Where are we going now, Mom?"

IVY CREEK

We'd only been in the car a short while when Aunt Dorace stopped in front of a huge house right next to a great big lake. In just a short time a very nice man and two ladies walked up. One lady was holding a leash with the cutest little black lab puppy you'd ever want to see. In fact, he reminded me of me when I was little. We walked over to another building where we met another lady. Mom introduced me to Uncle Jim, Aunt Judie, Aunt Julie and Aunt Karen.

Uncle Jim was the Director of Training at the guide dog school we were visiting-Ivy Creek. Aunt Karen was his assistant and Aunt Judie and Aunt Julie were puppy raisers for the school. The little black female guide puppy was Rain.

Uncle Jim told us how Ivy Creek was founded by a very generous couple who wanted to give back to a community that had given them so much. They also loved animals, especially labs, because of their superior temperament and keen intelligence. They decided to establish a school that would match worthy blind people with professionally trained guide dogs to provide them with better independence in their personal mobility and restore their dignity-just like Mom and me.

They contacted Uncle Jim to help them plan everything. They built climate-controlled kennels and a beautiful guesthouse for the student(s) to live in while in training.

Their dogs must pass intensive physical examinations, x-rays of their paws and legs and a special personality test before being considered for purchase. Then they are carefully matched with well-trained puppy raisers, where they will spend a year or more before returning to Uncle Jim and Aunt Karen to be professionally trained as an official guide dog. When thoroughly trained, they are given to a deserving blind person.

I followed Uncle Jim all over those grounds and was especially careful when we'd approach a step or uneven ground. Uncle Jim told Mom that he'd been watching me and I had "excellent guiding skills."

"Oh, shoot! 'Tain't nothing, Uncle Jim. I'm used to this stuff."

Mom promised Uncle Jim and the nice ladies that she'd talk to other blind folks about their school and tell them all about Ivy Creek. She did, too. Each time someone asked, she'd tell them about both Southeastern and Ivy Creek.

SCOUTING

It seems as though we'd just returned home and got unpacked when Mom got a phone call from some man in Goose
Creek. He was a scout leader and their motto for that month
was, "Walk a Mile in Their Shoes." The lady at the Association
for the Blind had given him our names and he wanted Mom
and me to come talk to his pack about being blind and having a
guide dog. Of course, Mom agreed.

"Uh, oh! Not that darned shedding blade again."

When we got to the Weapons Station, we had to relocate
to a bigger room to accommodate all the troops that showed up.
The auditorium was full of Boy Scouts, Girl Scouts, Cub Scouts
and Brownies Their moms and dads were even there, waiting
to hear Mom tell them all about *me*. Surprisingly, all those kids
were really good, too. Not one tried to pet me! They'd been instructed about that before we got there and they all remembered
what they'd been told. I was a little disappointed, especially
when Aunt Dorace told them that Riley wasn't working anymore and they could pet her.

"No fair, Mom! Riley gets all the attention and I
don't! No fair!"

Mom must have heard me, because once she finished answering all their questions, she removed my harness so I could play too.

✿

"Thanks, Mom! I love these kids and they love me! I love you too, Mom."

Between every couple of pets, I'd go back and give my mom one of my very special "I love you" licks. She'd smile and say,

"Good boy, little Sweet Potato! Very good boy."

We went to lots of other meetings that month. In fact, one man told Mom that they were making Riley and me honorary scouts.

"Hey, do I have to tie those funny looking knots in my tug rope? Does Riley have to sell cookies?"

UNCLE JD

Just before Easter Mom got an early morning telephone call.

" I wonder who that could be? This can't be good. It's too early. I haven't even eaten yet."

I could feel the sadness as it crept all over my mom. Tears began to stream down her cheeks as she listened to the voice on the receiver and drew me close to her. Uncle JD died.

Uncle JD was Mom's very, very special man friend for over 25 years. He was a giant of a man, but very gentle and very generous. He was smart, too. Right away, he told Mom that I was "so smart it is scary." I loved seeing Uncle JD and I loved the way he made my mom feel. Whenever he'd come down for a visit, I'd always find my very best toy and take it to him.

He'd just laugh and say,

"Hello, Appetite, (he called me appetite, but I don't know why), I don't want that old thing. I don't want nothing to do with you."

Then he'd kneel down and grab me and hold me tight. I'd squirm and finally get free, just to run right back up to him for more. He'd laugh again and say,

"You need to go get a rabbit."

I'd run go get my kong or my ball and we'd play for awhile. We'd go inside and he'd visit with Mom and I'd lay down on the floor next to their feet.

He always brought us lots of vegetables he'd grown on his farm. There would be enough to share with every family on our block!

Uncle JD must have really loved Tuesdays because anytime anyone would ask him when he was going to do something, he's always laugh and say,

"Tuesday. "

Uncle JD had only been sick for about 5 or 6 months and Mom was very sad when he died. I was too.

"Don't worry, Mom. I'll be the man in your life now."

Mom reached down and held me really close while she silently cried.

"He's with God in Heaven now, Little Sweet Potato," she said. "I wouldn't want to begrudge anyone an eternal place in my Father's Home, but I will surely miss him."

There were so many people at the funeral home we could hardly walk. I stayed really close to my mom and carefully guided her around all of them as they stood in groups. At last we got to the room where Uncle JD's body way lying. Folks were grabbing and hugging my Mom and then they'd just stand there, holding each other as they silently wept. I knew it was a very sad, somber occasion. I quietly sat right by my mom's leg, resting on her foot.

"I'll take care of you, Mom. Don't worry. Please try not to be sad. I'll take real good care of you. I promise."

Mom reached down and gently stroked my head with that very, very special loving touch that I'd grown to love so much.

The funeral was held in the church right across the street from Uncle JD's house. There were lots and lots of people there paying their respects. As soon as the service was over, we came straight back home.

Mom says there's a brighter star in the heavens now, watching over us. I think she just may be right. Sometimes she will hold me and laugh as she lovingly remembers something Uncle JD did or said. Mom loved him and, because she loved him, I did too.

"Farewell, Uncle JD. See ya Tuesday!"

WHAT'S NEXT?

We've been back to Columbia since talking with those "scout" people and going to Uncle JD;s funeral. Mom joined Uncle Jim and Aunt Angie on a special radio program, teaching folks about guide dogs, civil rights and what a sighted person should do when he sees a guide team. Tux and I just laid back and enjoyed the show.

We've been to a couple of other local meetings and Mom has spent a lot of time lately on another access issue problem. Mom calls it her "blind people stuff."

She stays busy planning Dixieland's special workshops, scheduled for November. Now, she's talking about starting another group called V.I.T.A.L. (Visually Impaired Talking, Answering, Listening) to provide peer support, education, information and an attentive ear to other blind folks. She's helping Aunt Tweety complete an application for Southeastern so she can get her very own guide dog, just like *me*.

Mom says we're going to Birmingham in July. I don't know where that is, but you can bet, I'm going to be right by her side.

Next week we're going camping again.

"All right, Mom! Camping! Let's go! Don't forget Zack's bag. Don't forget my kong. Don't forget my bones. Don't forget my Iams. I love you, Mom."

ZACK'S PAWS

This journal was lovingly written as a tribute to Aunt Dorace. Without her my mom would never have grown to become the person she is and would never have had the courage to do the things she's done; fight the battles she's won; or, most importantly, she would never have gotten the opportunity to get me. Aunt Dorace has been so supportive to my mom and the entire blind community, offering assistance whenever and wherever possible.

EPILOGUE

Currently there are around 28 million visually impaired and blind folks in the United States. Approximately 7000 of them use guide dogs. There are an estimated 14 guide dog schools through out this country that offer specially bred, professionally trained guide dogs to the blind community free of charge. They also provide the student with all tack, personal living accommodations, meals, and the necessary individual training to become a confident, responsible handler. Some even offer free transportation to and from the school. Others will pay for certain required medical expenses for the guide after the team returns home.

Why, then, are there so many blind Americans and so few guide teams? I think the answer stems from the lack of education. Most blind people just don't know what is available to them and they don't know where to get that information.

Some folks think only young, active people use guide dogs. Not so! Whether going across the world, to work or around the block, a professionally trained guide dog can provide a blind person with a renewed sense of dignity while giving him/her the ability to confidently maneuver independently and safely.

I know. Before God sent Zack into my life, I'd become a virtual vegetable-fearful of leaving the security of my own home. Now, I cannot imagine my life without him.

Together we've created a bond that has melded us forever. Zack is not a pet. He is not like a member of my family. He has become a part of me. He feels what I feel. We are one.

Thank you, God, for blessing me with my beloved Zack.